I0538150

Zombies

Incorporated

Nick Kisella

Based on the series by
Ryan Scott Weber

First Printing

A Weber Pictures Publication
Nick Kisella's photo by Stan Stronski
Ryan Scott Weber's photo by Michael Enoches

Dedications

For Nick:

Kim, always my love and best friend.
Nicholas Richard and Kimberly Gayle, our twin
babies.
Thanks Ryan, Tom, Joe, and the cast and crew
Here's another one Rich-
Special Thanks to Kevin and everyone at Chiller
Theatre.

For Ryan:

To my girlfriend Kristen for letting me pursue my
dream.
My best friend Tom Brady for all his hard work
and his family Lori and Bob for our amazing
location. To Joe, Brian, Steve, Taz, Jason, Nick,
and Doug. Thanks for the Hustle. Thanks also to
all the great people who came out and helped
make Zombies Inc. happen. We could not have
made Zombies Inc. without you guys.
Also to Kevin Clement for helping make my
dreams come true.

PROLOGUE

This group of stories, taken from Ryan Scott Weber's 'Zombies Inc.' series, predates the 'Mary Horror Saga' by at least two years. Shortly before the series and stories take place, a minor 'conventional' zombie outbreak had occurred in and around Bernardsville, NJ. When I say conventional, I mean one of the standard mainstays caused the outbreak: a virus, something toxic, a parasite or some other such tragic occurrence. I say this because during the 'Mary Horror Saga' there were zombies, but they were created through magic, black magic to be precise, and the people that had been 'turned' were not actually dead, more like 'possessed' and able to be returned to normal.

With that said- by all means continue on and enjoy the fun romp you'll get from Billy, Jimmy and Sheriff Tom!

TO THE
WINDBREAKERS!

Wally turned the camera on and began filming Billy and Jimmy. The camera zoomed in on them both. They were leaning against the wall at Jimmy's house. Both of them were wearing T-shirts but Jimmy had an American Flag draped over his shoulders. The pair looked as if they had just got out of bed.

"Did you wear underwear today?" Billy jokingly asked Jimmy.

"Yeah, I did," Jimmy replied, running fingers through his mess of light brown hair. "How about you?"

"Guys, we're rolling." Wally said just loud enough for them to hear.

"Oh, Oh," Billy said, standing up straighter and trying to look serious. "Hi, I'm Billy."

"And I'm Jim." Jimmy smiled.

"And since there's been a zombie outbreak, Jimmy and I were smart." Billy put his arm around Jimmy and pointed up with his free hand, smiling to emphasize how smart he and Jimmy were. "We decided to start our own zombie killing business."

"Yeah, fuck yeah!" Jimmy said making a fist enthusiastically.

"It's funny because, y'know, how we came up with the name. And they're filming us now." Billy gestured directly at the camera. "We usually film ourselves."

The camera cuts to a different scene from a few days earlier, when Billy had set the camera up and then positioned himself and Jimmy on the couch right in front of it. They were filming just for the sake of it, which they used to do for fun.

"I hope I look good in the camera." Jimmy started smoothing his hair down, trying not to feel embarrassed.

The television was on. Something on the news caught Billy's eye.

"Wait, hold on," he grabbed the remote and turned the volume up. "Who is that?"

"This is Chuck Marble reporting here in Bernardsville New Jersey. Sheriff Tom assures us that the zombie situation is under control, however experts say that there may still be more out there. Sheriff what is the latest?" He turned to Sheriff Tom and pointed the mike toward him.

"That's Sheriff Tom." Billy says, surprised.

"Is that really Sheriff Tom?"

Jimmy asked.

"Yeah. There's another zombie outbreak." Billy leaned back, mulling the situation over.

"Oh no," Jimmy said nervously.

"We've got the situation under control." Sheriff Tom said firmly, looking directly at Chuck Marble. "We're going to hunt down and kill every zombie." He turned toward the camera and pointed with a stern expression. "So I can assure you

that no one, no one, is in danger."

"This guy's an idiot!" Billy said with a laugh. "He's not going to be able to take care of the zombies."

"No," Jimmy said shaking his head, "No."

"What the hell? We can do it better than him." Billy pointed to them both and laughed. "Y;know what? We should start are own business."

"Yeah," Jimmy said, excited.

"And I got a great name."

"We can kill zombies." Billy looked surprised. "A name? Already?"

"Well yeah, I was just thinking-"

"Well what would we call it?" Billy asked, skeptically.

"Zombies Incorporated." Jimmy said smiling.

Billy had a sour look on his face. He shook his head, squinting. "Yeah, it involves zombies but we need a name."

The camera cuts back to the present.

"We understand each other." Jimmy gestured to Billy.

"Yeah, we can think what each other is thinking," He gestured to Jimmy, looking slightly confused, "when we're thinking it."

"Yeah." Jimmy agreed.

The camera shot returned to when Billy and Jimmy were trying to come up with a name.

"But I really like Zombies Incorporated." Jimmy said flat-out.

"We're gonna be incorporated, but we have to be-" Billy turned away, thinking hard.

"Well then listen to me." Jimmy said smacking him on the shoulder.

"But we need a name." Billy looked up thoughtfully. "Something that's gonna be awesome, and scream. So that we can get the ladies, we can be studs we can be rock stars. We can have a camera crew following us around." Billy's eyes lit up. "It would be awesome! We can be famous."

"I keep telling you," Jimmy threw his hands up, "Zombies Incorporated. It's an awesome name."

Billy just looked down mumbling, as if in deep though indecision.

"Wait!" Billy suddenly jumped in his seat. "Holy shit Jimmy, holy shit!" He wrapped his arm around Jimmy's neck and pulled him close, rubbing a closed fist over his hair excitedly. "I got it! I got the name!"

"Well, what is it?" Jimmy asked, pulling away.

"Zombies Incorporated!" He said with a big smile.

The camera cut to a shot of Jimmy standing alone with the flag still draped over his shoulders.

"Sometimes I really want to hit him really hard." Jimmy laughed.

The screen returned to the flashback.

"I know, cuz it was my idea." Jimmy said incredulously.

Billy snorted, giving Jimmy a double take.

"What do ya mean?" He said looking amazed. "You don't even talk! I don't get it. You don't say anything. All I hear is 'Ba bub bub ba, I'm hungry, ba bub bub ba fuck it." He comically imitated Jimmy.

Jimmy tried to get a word in but gave up.

"Okay let's get started. C'mon." Billy said, wild eyed, and acting like an old Italian talking with his hands. "We gotta get, we gotta post flyers so everyone can know we're around and we're gonna call like, a big television network and we're gonna get our own show."

Jimmy nodded and 'yeahed' Billy while he went on and on with flailing hands. When Billy was finally out of breath and quiet, Jimmy finally spoke up.

"Yeah, well that's a really good idea." Jimmy smiled and pointed to his stomach. "And you know something? My stomach's growling. I'm really hungry."

"Okay, okay." Billy relaxed and

smiled. "We'll go to Taco Bell and get something-"

"And then we'll hit Subway?" Jimmy said hopefully.

"Naw, subway sucks." Billy waved him off and got up from the couch.

"Does it?" Jimmy asked, annoyed that he wouldn't be able to get a 'Five dollar foot-long' again.

"C'mon, let's go." Billy looked back impatiently waiting for Jimmy to follow him.

The camera showed Billy and Jimmy leaning against the wall again. Billy rolled his eyes at the camera.

"I Think that, I think the zombies aren't going to be able to take this shit." Billy said casually. "Yeah, cuz we're gonna-"

"Yeah," Jimmy nodded vigorously, cutting Billy off. "Cuz we're gonna stick it, and we're not gonna pull out."

The camera flicks off and on and we see Billy and Jimmy sitting at a bar.

"What the hell are we even gonna use to kill these zombies if we ever even get a phone call?" Billy was flabbergasted, and more than a little annoyed that they hadn't received a call yet. He looked down at his cell phone and shook his head.

"A lemon." Jimmy laughed.

"A lemon?" He quirked up his

brow and stared at Jimmy as if he was offended. "What the hell are we gonna do? Burn the shit out of their eyes with it? I mean, what the hell are you talking about?" He waved a hand at Jimmy dismissively. "We'd have a better chance of choking the shit out of them. Where the hell did that come from?"

"Oh I dunno," He grinned. "Y'know, I was watching a cooking show."

The camera flicked to Billy standing alone in a hallway near the 'Men's Room' of the bar.

"Don't tell Jimmy this," He whispered. "But he's a really bad cook."

The camera went right back to the two of them sitting at the bar.

"Ah, y'know food, I don't get it." Billy turned away.

"I saw a guy, he was cutting a lemon, and I'll tell ya-"

Jimmy was interrupted by the sound of Billy's phone ringing.

Billy jumped, eyes widening with excitement.

"Uh wait, hold on," He pointed to the phone. "I got a phone call. Hey we got one! Holy shit we got one!" He held himself and took a deep breath. "I'm nervous."

The camera cut right to Billy, alone in what looked to be some sort of barn. He had a dark bandana folded and wrapped around his head.

"Jimmy and I, we got our first zombie call." He said quickly, staring directly into the camera. "And I was so nervous. I hoped that I could handle it well." He said breathlessly.

The picture returned to Billy and Jimmy at the bar.

"Who's it from?" Jimmy asked looking at the phone.

"I don't know! Phone says it's restricted." Billy replied, sweating and nervously out of breath. "Holy shit, here we go," he whispered, raising the phone to his ear to answer it.

"Hello, Zombies Incorporated, this is Billy." He said in a rush.

Jimmy watched him, half waiting for him to hyperventilate.

"Oh," Billy said into the phone, sitting up and sounding confident.

"You don't say. Okay, we'll be right there." Billy clicked the phone off, dropped it on the bar and held his heads in his hands. "Oh shit."

"What?" Jimmy asked.

"It was a girl." He said. "A damsel in distress." He looked directly in the camera and pointed. "We got a call. Our first zombie call."

"Alright!" Jimmy grinned, excited.

"Okay let's go!" Billy fist pumped. "To the windbreakers!"

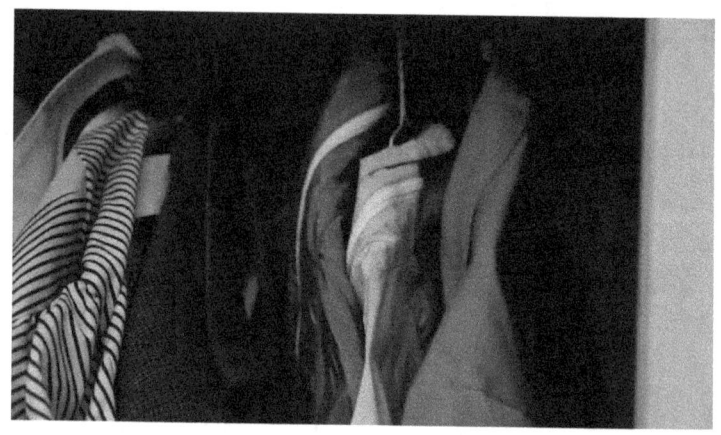

The two of them went back to Billy's house where they kept their uniforms, which consisted of two windbreakers; Jimmy's was yellow, and Billy's was green. Each had a zippered collar pocket that held a hood. The pair put their respective jacket on and then each wrapped a bandana around their heads.

Jimmy looked in a mirror and pointed at it as if he had guns in his hands.

Billy stared in a mirror when he was done.

"You fuckin' hot, sexy bitch," he said to himself before heading out to his minivan with Jimmy.

The camera wavered around a bit until Wally was able to get into the backseat of the van. He had the camera focused straight ahead, between Billy, who was driving, and Jimmy, in the front passenger seat.

Billy was buckling his seatbelt when he turned to the camera.

"Ladies and gentlemen, we are on our first zombie call." He was breathing heavy, still nervous. "We got a call from a damsel in distress. Right Jimmy?" He looked over at his partner. "You ready?"

"Yeah, I'm fuckin' ready!" Jimmy clenched a fist, thoroughly psyched.

"Yeah, we're ready to battle some zombies! With our training from the Zombie Academy, we will defeat the zombie, and with the help of Sheriff Tom."

"You're gonna call him?" Jimmy sounded surprised.

"Yeah." Billy pulled out his phone.

"Well alright, here." He held a walkie-talkie out for Bille. "Let me turn it on."

"It's a nine-seven-six number isn't it?" Billy saw the walkie-talkie and grinned, snatching it up and putting his phone back in his pocket. "Oh, yeah, thanks."

"Is it working?" He asked Billy.

"Yeah, it's on." He said, holding it up. "Sheriff Tom! Come in Sheriff Tom."

The camera flickered to a shot of Sheriff Tom, standing next to his car. There was a disclaimer flashing across the bottom of the screen.

Sheriff Tom's scene is a dramatization created after the show for effect only.

The Sheriff is listening to Jazz, dancing next to his car. "It's all good," he said, smiling. He didn't even acknowledge that Billy was calling him.

The camera goes back to Billy.

"Well, I hope he comes." Billy put the radio down and started the van.

The camera moves to show Sheriff Tom in the same barn where Billy was shown before. He was still in uniform.

"I had my, I was singing to my favorite, I was jamming to my favorite tune. What's that? Z.I. or something like that." Sheriff Tom nodded and smiled. "It was really blasting. I was having a good time out there. Then this call comes in, and I'm thinking to myself, I'd like to finish my song first. Naturally I waited until I finished my song and then I picked up the call and obviously who was there? The two numbskulls." He shook his head, annoyed but grinning.

The shot goes back to Billy and Jimmy in the minivan. Billy is still struggling to maneuver the minivan around the other cars in the driveway.

"Let's go." Jimmy said as his partner finally pulled the minivan out into traffic.

"We have no idea what we're doing do we?" Billy said, half serious.

"No we don't." Jimmy agreed with a chuckle.

"How about Sheriff Tom? You

think he's actually gonna show up?"

"I hope he does." Jimmy looked out the window to see if he could see the Sheriff's car.

"Hold on, I've got problems." Billy made a face, then farted loudly.

The camera goes back to just Billie in the barn.

"Y'know, every time we're driving in the van, Jimmy farts. We could be anywhere. Now I don't say anything, but it smells terrible in that van." He had a serious look on his face.

The camera cuts to Jimmy in the barn.

"I don't know, there's a weird smell in Billy's van. I don't know what it is. I think he just farts a lot." Jimmy shook his head, looking grossed out.

The shot goes back to Billy and Jimmy in the minivan.

"Man, it's always difficult to get

out of this driveway." Billy said, getting the van on the road. "We are on our way, to defeat the zombie." Billy turned to say in the camera. "We are making history in Bernardsville today." He said dramatically. "Right Jimmy?"

"Yeah!" He shouted.

The camera goes to Jimmy in the barn alone.

"I mean, we'd be driving around and he always gets lost. He

doesn't even know how to drive, I don't think." Jimmy said seriously.

The camera returns to the van. They're finally driving down the road.

"Jimmy," Billy asked, looked from left to right as he drove.

"Yeah?"

"I don't know where the hell we are." He said, frustrated, squinting to see.

"I don't know." Jimmy agreed.

The camera changes to show Sheriff Tom listening to smooth Jazz, driving casually down the road as if he hasn't a care in the world.

Sheriff Tom's scene is a dramatization created after the show for effect only.

The view goes back to Billy driving the minivan. He's ducked down trying to figure out where they are when his eyes suddenly widen after catching sight of something.

"I think this is it." He said, slowly looking around.

"Alright!" Jimmy said.

"Yeah, this is it." He said, not quite as certain as he sounded, but excited and nervous at the same time. He pulled into an empty unpaved lot. It was covered in stones and bordered by woods. Billy pointed off in the distance where there was a path. "I think we have to go through there."

He pulled the minivan up to the end of the lot, close to the woods. "Okay. Let's go!" He said looking at Jimmy.

They both got out of the van and ran toward the woods. Wally trailed along, the camera jumping and swerving as he ran to keep up with them.

"Where is this bitch?" Billy said, gasping and falling behind Jimmy. He was clearly annoyed at the distance they had to travel to reach her. "This running shit sucks," he thought, pushing harder to try to keep up with Jimmy.

He didn't see the tree root sticking out of the ground until it was too late. Billy fell flat, twisting his leg under him.

Jimmy saw him fall and ran back to get him.

"Are you alright?" He asked.

"My leg. I think I hurt my leg."

Billy said struggling to get up. For a minute there on the ground he felt like a turtle trapped on its back, unable to get his bearings, body not moving the way he wanted it to. "Help me up." He said to Jimmy. Where the fuck is Sheriff Tom?" He said, getting to his feet with Jimmy's help.

"You okay now?" Jimmy asked.

"I think I hurt my back." Billy said. He put his arm over Jimmy's shoulder and the two struggled on through the woods. "That fall was bad."

A short distance away there was a barn.

"Let me try something." Jimmy said before they reached it. "Let me fix it."

He stood behind Billy and put his arms around him. Without warning and grunting with effort, Jimmy lifted Billy up, successfully cracking his back.

Billy sighed in unbelievable relief.

"You have the right touch." Billy moaned happily, eyes closed in bliss.

"Is that the barn." Jimmy pointed to it.

Billy blinked open his eyes and smiled.

"So this IS it." He said, thankful that he wasn't as lost as he really thought he was. "We're here! We found it Wally. Yeah."

The barn was the customary red and enormous, with double doors right in front of them. They were open wide, and though there were stalls visible, neither of them saw any horses.

"C'mon Wally." Jimmy said looking into the camera.

"Yeah, great." Wally nodded, the camera moving slightly.

Jimmy walked closer to the entrance of the barn. It was a wide opening. He couldn't see anyone inside.

"Let's go inside." He said, coming up behind Jimmy. "I bet this is where the zombie is!"

"I think so." Jimmy agreed.

"And that girl called me from here. That's where she called me from." Billy pointed to the phone hanging inside the door.

"I don't know why the fuck I took this job." Wally muttered nearly inaudible in the background.

"Yeah, where is he?" Billy whispered.

"I don't know," Jimmy blurted out.

"I'm scared." Billy muttered under his breath.

"I am too." Jimmy said, staying next to Billy.

"I hear your balls tingling."

Billy joked.

Suddenly, there was a noise in one of the stalls ahead of them. They all stopped dead when they heard it.

Billy's blood ran cold.

"Uh oh," Wally whispered, ready to run if it became necessary.

They heard a moaning.

"Holy shit!" Billy said. "What the fu-"

Before he could finish cursing a hand came out of the stall opening. It grabbed onto the framework. The creature's skin was tinged with shades of gray and looked so dry it was nearly leathery.

A second later the rest of him staggered out into the open, and Billy and Jimmy saw their first real zombie up close.

He was tall, wearing a dark t-shirt, jeans and boots. He had long wavy hair that fluttered around his shoulder each time his feet shuffled.

"Holy shit!" Billy said, terrified. "There he is, there he is!"

The zombie had been looking in the opposite direction when he moved into the open, and continued on in that direction, away from Billy and Jimmy.

Wally heard a car door slam outside. He silently prayed that it was who he thought it was, and took that as his cue to momentarily abandon ship for who he hoped was their savior. He seriously doubted that Billy and Jimmy would confront the zombie on their own anyway, or at least he hoped they wouldn't.

Sure enough, when he got outside he saw Sheriff Tom approaching the barn from his car.

He let the camera continue to film, focusing in on Sheriff Tom as he approached the barn.

"I just got a call from those two dimwits," Sheriff Tom said staring right into the camera. "They think that there's something going on in this barn."

There was shouting coming from the barn, and a sudden scream from a female. Confident, Sheriff Tom continued to walk casually to the barn, while Wally picked up the pace, wanting to get whatever was happening on film before the Sheriff came in a saved the day for them all.

Wally got inside just in time to

see the zombie walking into another stall. The woman screaming was on the ground in a corner, trying to protect herself with her arms over her face.

Billy and Jimmy followed the zombie inside, staying a short distance behind him.

"There she is Jimmy!" Billy shouted. "Let's get the zombie!"

Billy ran up behind the zombie and grabbed his shoulder. The creature turned around and snarled at him, suddenly lunging toward Billy. He grabbed the zombie by the throat with both hands, turning away from the bloody face and bulging eyes of the creature. It snapped at him, trying to pull closer so he could bite Billy.

"Get him in the stomach Jimmy, get him in the stomach!" Billy shouted, crazed, struggling to keep the zombie off.

Jimmy tried to hit the zombie in the stomach but was firmly pushed aside by Sheriff Tom, who had just entered the stall.

Sheriff Tom shot the zombie in the head.

"Asshole!" He shouted at the fallen zombie.

The camera switched to Sheriff Tom sitting in the barn alone again. He was grinning at the camera.

"I fired one shot," Sheriff Tom

smile, and jokingly blew air into the barrel of his pistol, "and that was all she wrote." He nodded to the camera. "It's all good."

The scene changed back to the stall in the barn.

Wally panned the camera around the stall, showing the cringing woman finally able to stand up, but still clearly shaken by the entire situation, and the zombie, lying prone on the ground.

Then he lost control of his bladder.

"We got that motherfucker!" Billy shouted, sounding elated. He started to walk away from the body and smacked Jimmy on the shoulder. "Good job Jimmy! We got him!"

"I think it was just me and you." Jimmy said, waving a hand at Sheriff Tom as he walked away. "I don't know what he's sellin', but it was me and you."

"Yeah, we did it!" Billy declared. "We got the zombie. That's what we tell the press." He pointed at Jimmy, determined. "We got the zombie, we got the balls!"

"Hey where's the girl." Jimmy was looking all over the stall, not noticing her slip away a few minutes earlier. "I want her number."

"Uh, who knows?" Billy said, seeing her run out of the barn a second later. "We'll get it next time."

The camera flickered and the scene was suddenly of the girl that called Billy and Jimmy to begin with. She was sitting alone on an overturned bucket in the center of a stall in the barn. She held one of Billy and Jimmy's 'Zombies Inc.' flyers and nervously tapping her foot.

Holly was in her mid-twenties, with long dark hair that was braided into a ponytail. Her dark eyes darted around nervously. It was if she expected another zombie to come jumping out from somewhere at any moment. She was still clearly shaken and fearful.

"Um, so you were just saved by, uh, Sheriff Tom, or was it Billie and Jimmy. I'm not really too clear on that." Wally asked her, zooming in on her face.

"Uh, I'm not really sure." She held her hands out, still holding the flyer in one of them. "They all just kind of ran in and they, the two guys that I called, they were strangling him."

"We actually have a surprise here for you. There's someone here to see you." Wally said happily. "To say 'hi'."

"Hi," Jimmy said walking over to her. "I saved you."

"Uh, hi," The girl said, smiling.

Jimmy turned around and sat on

her lap. "I really want your number." He sounded excited.

"Yeah, okay." She replied, laughing as he sat on her.

"I was telling Wally about you." He gestured to the camera and smiled.

"Yeah he's been talking about you, uh all weekend." Wally said. "He told me all about you and I just think you guys have a lot in common. Holly, what's your sign?"

"Um, Virgo?" She sounded uncertain and grinned, looking a little uncomfortable as Jimmy put his hand on her head and began running his fingers through her hair.

"Well, that's uh-" Jimmy look slightly taken aback by her response, but continued to rub her hair and then smooth it out. It looked like he was petting a dog or a cat.

"Uh, that's nice." Wally laughed watching Jimmy. "Yeah

that's nice, pet her."

The camera switched back to the moments after the zombie was shot, with Jimmy and Billy walking out of the barn.

"I wish I'd gotten her phone number." Jimmy said again as they walked out into the open air. It was getting late, darkness falling.

"Now where the hell did we leave the car?" Billy asked, looking around.

"I don't know buddy." He said.

"We gotta go." Billy said seriously, "Because the bar is closing soon. It's getting' dark."

"Yeah. Where's Sheriff Tom? He totally left us." Jimmy looked around, disappointed.

"Holy fuck," Wally muttered, realizing how he must look.

"Ah Wally, you peed your pants again!" Billy looked at Wally.

"Oh my god," Wally whispered.

"What's that stain?" Jimmy looked at Wally, not realizing what happened.

The camera changed to Billy sitting along in the barn again. He looked directly in the camera, and though he wanted to look serious, you could see that he was having a difficult time keeping a straight face.

"When Wally peed his pants, y'know, I really," He looked up searching for words. "It was natural for me. It's like, y'know, you should really always be able to pee where ever you want."

The picture cut back to Billy and Jimmy outside the barn again.

"Don't feel bad Wally." Billy tried to keep a straight face. "Did I ever tell you I have a condition called a burnin' in the urine'?"

"Urine burnin'?" Wally asked skeptically.

"Why do you keep tellin'

people this shit?" Jimmy walked over to Billy looking annoyed.

"Because I want them to feel bad for me." Billy grinned.

"Well, fuck that." Jimmy laughed.

"We did it. We got our first zombie!" Billy changed the subject and high-fived Jimmy.

"Yeah, alright." Jimmy hugged his partner in triumph and laughed.

"We've got to alert the press,

and we gotta go get a beer." Billy laughed turning away to try to find the minivan with Jimmy close behind.

"I'm really not getting paid enough for doing this shit." Waller mumbled.

The scene changed back to Jimmy sitting on Holly's lap.

"Well Jimmy, she's clearly into you, so where do you think you'd take her on your first date?" Wally asked.

"Um, I don't know," He stared off, "maybe McDonalds, I'm thinkin'."

Holly was a second away from laughing out loud at what Jimmy had said.

"Holly looks like she loves that idea." Wally said, joking with Holly, but Jimmy thought he was serious.

"Yeah, it'll be great," Holly chuckled, "Really great."

"And then we'll go to a strip

club. Maybe get some lap dances."
Jimmy continued.

"Just as long as it's a classy place." Holly started laughing.

"Oh, okay." Jimmy said. "Classy. Oh, then we have to go to New York."

The view cut to the bar.

Billy and Jimmy were holding full shot glasses. By their expressions they had already downed a few.

"Okay. We just did a great job Jimmy." Billy's words were a bit slurred. He raised his glass. "We got our first zombie."

"Well Billy, its one down." Jimmy slurred as well as they toasted and downed their shots.

Sheriff Tom walked past them.

"Is that Bald Britney?" Billy asked, his head spinning a bit.

"No, that's Sheriff Tom." Jimmy said. "He's always fuckin' around.

The camera cut to Sheriff Tom. He was sitting at the bar.

"What the hell's this guy doing, calling me 'Bald Britney'?" Sheriff Tom said, annoyed. "Well you know what? One day, you mark my words, they're gonna be doing a TV show about good old Sheriff Tom." He said adamantly.

The camera went back to Billy and Jimmy.

"He's watchin' what we're doin'." Jimmy shook his head.

"You think he's following us?" Billy asked.

"Yeah."

"I hope it's not Bald Britney because she gave me, I think it was crabs or a burnin' in my urine." Billy sipped a fresh glass of beer.

"Did she really?" Jimmy sipped a beer of his own.

"Yep." He nodded. "A burnin' in my urine."

"Yeah? That's a problem." Jimmy laughed.

"You got burnin' urine?" Billy joked.

"No, I don't have that problem."

"You ever have a pop a loop a

dupa?" Billy laughed.

"No, I don't have that problem either." Jimmy laughed.

The camera panned to Sheriff Tom again.

"I saw Billy and Jimmy on the news and you know what? They had a tough day, so you know what? Let's give them the credit for it. Even though it just took me one shot," he blew into the barrel of his pistol again and grinned, "to take care of business."

The camera flashed to the news. Chuck Marble stood wearing a crisp suit outside with Billy and Jimmy standing behind him.

"Well Bernardsville, it looks like we have a type of zombie squad out there taking care of the town zombie problems to my left and my right." He nodded to Jimmy and Billy, who were only a moment ago making faces and flailing their arms behind him like teenagers. "I'm here with the founders, owners more or less, of Zombies Incorporated. Guys, what led you to start Zombies Inc.?"

"Well, Chuck, we were in our underwear one day and we just thought of it." Billy said smiling and being silly in front of the camera.

"Is that right?" Chuck asked, putting the mike in front of Jimmy.

"Yeah me and Jimmy were both in our fucking underwear." Jimmy grinned and rubbed the back of Chuck's head.

"Yeah and Jimmy has glow in the dark underwear." Billy laughed.

"Yeah, well he has leopard ones." Jimmy retorted smiling.

"And zebra's." Billy chimed in.

"What about your thong?" Jimmy laughed.

"You're not supposed to tell anybody about the thing." Billy said angrily.

"I'm sorry, I didn't know-"

"Well guys, I'm sure that Bernardsville wants to know: how are the zombie calls going guys?" Chuck asked, trying to steer things a little more seriously.

"Oh, they're fuckin' dead."

Jimmy said.

"Dead, dead and more dead motherfuckers." Billy said loudly into the mike smiling.

"Really dead motherfuckers." Jimmy added before Chuck took the mike back.

"I'm sure that our whole town is great with you swearing on our airwaves." Chuck said, trying to make light of it.

"We're not allowed to swear?"

Billy asked.

"No, I'm afraid not." Chuck shook his head.

"What do you mean were not supposed to fucking swear?" Jimmy complained.

Billy started cracking up.

"Well anyway, in Bernardsville our zombie problem is solved."

Billy grabbed the mike from Chuck and grabbed Jimmy, pulling him in front of the newscaster.

"Jimmy, I know you're emotional right now," Billy pulled him closer as he mock-cried while Chuck was trying to get his mike back, "but I want to tell America, that if you've got a zombie problem, you call Zombies Incorporated!"

A NEW TV SHOW FROM RYAN SCOTT WEBER
RYAN SCOTT WEBER TOM BRADY JOE PARASCAND
BILLY AND JIMMY'S
ZOMBIES
INCORPORATED
BUSINESS IS DEAD
FALL 2013

Nick Kisella grew up in Manville, New Jersey,

 where he began writing fantasy and horror while attending high school. Some of his first published work appeared in the Indie magazines 'Dreadknight', and 'The Nocturnal Lyric'. Since then his work has appeared in various forms from print and online magazines to blogs. His first fantasy novel, 'The Emerald and the Blade' came out in 1989 by a long defunct publisher, with 'The Chalice of Souls' soon to follow. Some of his more recent work includes a screenplay and novelization for 'Nifty

Entertainment' a California based Indie production company, as well as getting the first two fantasy novels he wrote as a teen, 'The Chalice of Souls' and 'Death and the Doomweaver' back in print for the sheer nostalgia of it.

'Morningstars', his first full-length horror novel was published by Black Bed Sheet Books in 2012. 'The Beasts and the Walking Dead' a post-apocalyptic fiction novel, has also been published by Black Bed Sheet Books and is the first part of a series. The second book in that series, 'Under Construction' is actually a prequel, published in October of 2013. He wrote the novelization to the James Balsamo film, 'I Spill Your Guts', and recently finished the novelization for the Ryan Scott Weber films, 'Mary Horror', and 'Sheriff Tom versus the Zombies'. His latest work with Weber Films is the novelization of the reality series, 'Zombies Inc.'.

Always having an eventful life, he writes when time allows, usually after dark.

A fitness enthusiast, he has been a certified fitness instructor involved in the industry for twenty years, and continues to stay in shape and train individuals while in his late 40s.

Nick resides in rural Northwestern New Jersey with his wife and twins.

Ryan Scott Weber (Born February 24, 1980) is an American film director, writer, screenwriter, producer, cinematographer, actor, editor and musician. He shoots and produces many of his films in his native town of Bernardsville, New Jersey. Ryan began his interest in filmmaking at just 15 years old with an old VHS camcorder. Now, at the age of 33, he is the owner of Weber Pictures Company in New Jersey. Weber also plays the drums and has released two albums with the Trustkill Records band Crash Romeo in 2004 and 2008. For almost 15 years now he is still directing, editing, writing, producing, acting, drumming and shooting. Weber has a distinctive directorial style. He manages to make what look like big budget movies for little money. Weber's first feature film, Mary Horror, was released in 2012 and the sequel Sheriff Tom Vs. The Zombies was completed in April 2013. He is currently wrapping up the third film of the trilogy "Witches Blood" for a 2014 release. Weber's latest project is "Zombies Incorporated". Where he takes characters from his other films and puts them into a reality style TV show. Weber is a strong supporter of independent film and the conventions that are involved in this surrounding. Weber and his crew have attended and ventured over twenty conventions in the last year and a half. The Chiller Theatre Convention in Parsippany, NJ featured the film Mary Horror and also Sheriff Tom Vs. The Zombies with two exclusive showings. Weber will continue to make independent films and ensures us the best in yet to come!

www.ingramcontent.com/pod-product-compliance
Lightning Source LLC
Chambersburg PA
CBHW071628140626
46555CB00021B/1252